The Hopeville Book of Records

by Michelle Murray-Cox

illustrated by John Yahyeh

Blake
EDUCATION
Better ways to learn

Characters

 Katy

Mason

 Miss Spencer

Contents

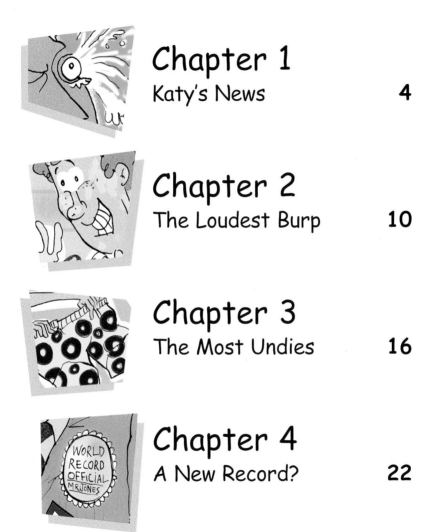

Chapter 1
Katy's News 4

Chapter 2
The Loudest Burp 10

Chapter 3
The Most Undies 16

Chapter 4
A New Record? 22

Katy's News

"A lady in England can whistle 'Twinkle, Twinkle Little Star' through her nose and a man in America can shoot milk out of his eyeballs!"

It was news day. Katy had brought her brand-new *Book of World Records* to share with the class.

"Thank you, Katy. I think that is enough," said her teacher, Miss Spencer.

At lunchtime, Katy and her best friend, Mason, looked through the book.

"I'm going to set a world record and get my name in this book," said Katy. "Then I'll be famous."

"Me too," said Mason.

"Mum says I burp louder than anyone in the world," boasted Katy.

"I can make the world's tallest ice-cream," boasted Mason.

Their friend Luke heard them talking. "I bet I can break a world record too," he said.

"Great!" said Katy. "Let's all do it at the Community Hall on Saturday. Anyone who wants to break a world record can come along."

Chapter 2

The Loudest Burp

Miss Spencer agreed to help. The class
made posters to put up around town.

Luke's father was the editor of the *Hopeville News*. He put an ad in the newspaper.

Word soon got around the little town of Hopeville.

On Saturday, the whole town was at the Community Hall — even the mayor!

Miss Spencer pinned up a large sheet of paper for the results.

Katy went first. She took a big sip of
fizzy soft drink. She swallowed hard.
Katy opened her mouth, and let out a
HUGE burp.

It echoed off the walls of the hall.

"How loud?" asked Katy.

"21 decibels," said Miss Spencer. "That's very loud but the world's loudest burp was over 100 decibels."

The Most Undies

Then it was Mason's turn.

"My mum wouldn't let me bring the ice-cream," said Mason. "She said it would melt."

"So I brought these." Mason put his hand into his backpack and pulled out a pair of shiny boxer shorts.

"Mason, they're your undies," said Katy. Everyone giggled.

"I know. I am going to wear the most underwear that anyone has ever worn at one time," Mason said. He pulled on the boxer shorts over his jeans.

Then he put on a big, white pair of his
dad's jockey shorts. Next came a pair of
bright orange and green undies, and then a
pair covered in racing cars.

When Mason put on a pair of his mum's pink, frilly underpants, she ran over and grabbed Mason by the left ear. She marched him right out of the hall.

"Five pairs of underpants," said Miss Spencer.

"Six, if you count the ones he had on under his jeans," said Katy.

"That's a lot," said Miss Spencer.

"But it's not a world record," said Katy sadly.

Chapter 4

A New Record?

The mayor tried to blow the world's biggest bubble. He was doing well. But then Jake came off his skateboard trying to do 100 ollies in a row. They both ended up covered in a sticky, pink mess.

By the end of the day people had tried everything — doing cartwheels, eating worms, spitting watermelon seeds, jumping on pogo sticks and going cross-eyed. The result sheet was full, but not one world record had been broken.

The whole town was sad. Not Miss Spencer!
She was smiling!

"Why are you so happy, Miss Spencer?"
asked Katy. "We didn't break a single
record."

"Oh yes we did," said Miss Spencer. "When you came up with this idea, I phoned the people at the *Book of World Records*."

"They said we could set a record for the most people in one town trying to break a world record. This is Mr Jones from the *Book of World Records.*"

Mr Jones shook Katy's hand. "Well done, Katy. Thanks to you, Hopeville will be in the next edition of the *Book of World Records*. It will be a hard record to beat."

"95 people tried to break a record here today. Hopeville has a population of 100 people. That's 95 percent of the town's population," said Mr Jones.

Everyone cheered. The town of Hopeville was in the *Book of World Records* and would be famous for a very long time.

ad
a notice that tells people about something

boasted
bragged, talked proudly

boxer shorts
loose underpants that look like shorts

decibels
used to measure the loudness of sound

edition

printed copies of a book; when copies are printed again, with changes, it is called a new edition

editor

a person who looks after a newspaper

ollies

skateboarding tricks where the skateboard and rider go in the air

population

the number of people who live in a place

Michelle Murray-Cox

Did you know? The tallest living person is 2·35 metres tall, the shortest living person is 65 cm tall (short) and the longest ear hair is 13·2 cm! World records are amazing. I got the idea to write this book from my son. He and his friends are always doing crazy things that make me giggle.

John Yahyeh

Elizabeth Best

Elizabeth Best writes a bit of everything ... adult short stories, children's stories, plays, articles and novels.
Best of all though, she enjoys writing stories for children. It is pure joy!

Cliff Watt

I started illustrating after I became shipwrecked on a desert island. It was very difficult at first, but soon I learnt to use everything. This book was drawn with a burnt bone from last night's dinner.

furiously
unstoppable energy

I beg your pardon
a polite way of
saying sorry

puzzled
to think about
a problem

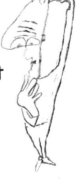

wolfing
to eat very quickly

GLOSSARY

awful
very bad

bellowed
shouted loudly

dashed
ran quickly

envious
to want what
someone else has

"That cat food looks nice," said Mrs Gladys McTavish.